Lodu's Escape

and Other Stories from Africa

Phoebe Mugo, Editor

Friendship Press • New York

Editorial Offices:
475 Riverside Drive, Room 860, New York, NY 10115

Distribution Offices:
P.O. Box 37844, Cincinnati, OH 45222-0844

Friendship Press gratefully acknowledges the permission granted by Central Tanganyika Press in Dodoma, Tanzania, to publish the English version of *The Red Kitenge,* and by Asempa Publishers in Accra, Ghana, to publish the English version of *A Match Against Juju.* These stories were written in a workshop organized by several Christian publishers in Africa in 1984. The teachers were Mabel Segun of Nigeria and Marion Van Horne of the United States. The project was funded by the World Association for Christian Communication and coordinated by Phoebe Mugo, editor of this book.

Map by Ruth Soffer
Layout and typesetting by Carol Gorgun

Manufactured in the United States of America

Library of Congress Cataloging-in-Publication Data

Lodu's escape and other stories from Africa / edited by Phoebe Mugo.
    p.   cm.
    Contents: Lodu's escape—Thoko's visit—The red kitenge—A match against Juju—Kalulu's cave—Elaine's African Christmas.
    ISBN 0-377-00269-0
    1. Africa—Juvenile fiction. 2. Children's stories, African (English) [1. Africa—Fiction. 2. Short stories.]
PZ5.L754 1994
[Fic]—dc20
                                    93-44799
                                          CIP
                                          AC

Contents

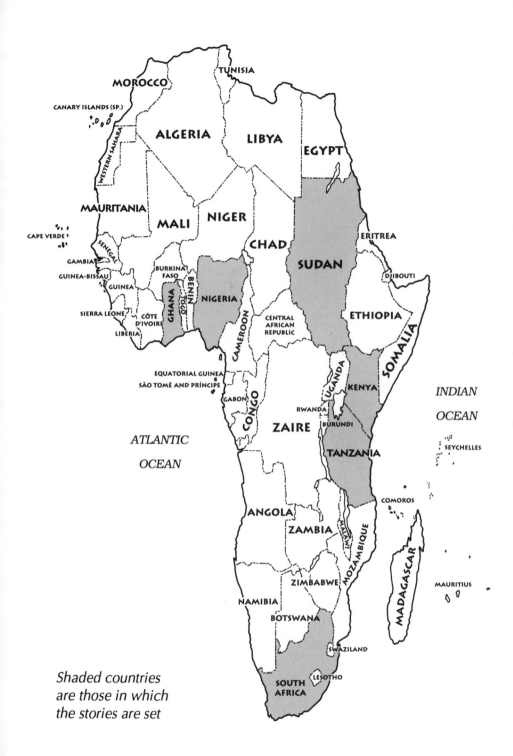

Shaded countries
are those in which
the stories are set

Lodu's Escape

Gordon Tikiba

"Mother, I can't understand what's going on! During the day we're shelled with big guns. They go on shooting through the night. Can't we go to the church compound?" Lodu asked. "Many people have already gone there."

Kaku listened very carefully to her twelve-year-old son. She also was beginning to feel afraid. It seemed this war would never end in Sudan. Lodu's father had been killed by a bullet at night. Since then Kaku had cared for Lodu alone. She decided that he was right. They must leave their village.

In their small hut, Kaku spread a torn blanket on the ground. She carefully heaped their few belongings on the blanket. Meanwhile, Lodu went about looking for what he could take with them. He came back into the hut with an axe and a short-handled hoe. These are very useful tools, he thought to himself. He put them into the bundle his mother was tying.

To get from Muniki to the church compound was not an easy thing. People who walked along the main road often were searched for weapons. People were forbidden to carry spears, bows and arrows, even axes.

But Lodu knew of a path that passed behind a big hill in the distance, and then joined the main road at Nyakuran. This way he and his mother could reach the church compound without being stopped at roadblocks. He told his mother about his plan.

"Do you want us to be killed?" his mother exclaimed. "That path has been laid with mines! Anybody who walks along it is likely to be blown up."

Lodu refused to listen to his mother's warning. He had seen many people killed by bullets and hunger too. He wanted to walk along that path.

Late that afternoon Lodu persuaded his mother to take the risk. Looking fearful, she put the bundle on her head. He went ahead, carrying a long bamboo pole. As they walked, he beat the grass in front of him, hoping to explode any booby traps that might have been laid along the path.

Everything went well for a while, and Kaku began to feel better. Suddenly there was an explosion. "Boom! Boom!" The bamboo had hit one of the traps. Fortunately, neither Lodu nor Kaku was hurt. Lodu's plan had worked!

"Mother, don't be afraid," he said. "We'll get to the main road soon and then we'll be able to walk straight to the church compound."

Lodu spoke bravely, but he was worried. He and his mother had not eaten any good food for more than three months. They had depended on leaves and wild fruits. As they walked, he couldn't help asking, "Will we find something to eat at the church?"

Kaku was silent for a while before she could answer her son. "I don't know, Lodu. I hear the people at the church are kind. Even if we don't get food there, we'll be safe. I will be glad to meet some friends and stay in one place."

Lodu was not happy with his mother's answer. He was very hungry and wanted something to eat.

Soon they came to the main road, but it was deserted. This was strange. Usually this late in the day many people would be walking back home. Fearing that something was wrong, Lodu and his mother decided to walk the remaining distance along village paths. Another hour of walking brought them to the gate of the church. Looking into the compound, Lodu saw many people. It was so crowded! What had happened?

A man sitting at the gate got up to greet them. "I am Pastor Amosa," he said. "You are welcome to the church compound. Please tell me your names, and where you are coming from."

Although Lodu felt tired, he stood politely and gave Pastor Amosa their names. The pastor explained that all the people had run away from their homes because of nearby fighting the previous night. Kaku took the bundle from her head and sank to the ground, wondering what would become of them.

The pastor understood. "Lodu," he said, "you look weak. I think you've not eaten anything for many days. Go and sit with the children. I'll see that you get some porridge."

Lodu was more than happy. In one corner of the compound he could see three big drums steaming with porridge. He walked over to where the children were, and soon began to make friends. He told them about the long walk, the dangerous path, the exploding land mine. They told him about the fighting that they had escaped, too.

Just then Pastor Amosa began to arrange the children in lines. "Do you have any container for your porridge?" he asked Lodu.

"Yes, I do," answered Lodu.

He quickly ran to his mother. She took an old bowl from the bundle and gave it to him.

"I'm going to call out your names," Pastor Amosa told the children. "When you hear your name, go and be given some porridge."

Lodu was very happy. As soon as he received his portion, he sat down, put his bowl before him, and began scooping up the porridge with his fingers.

Children sat everywhere, eating joyfully. There was a lot of noise. Pastor Amosa looked at them, but felt happy only for a moment. He was very worried, because he knew this was the last of the porridge.

"If there is no flight from Nairobi bringing in more maize flour," he thought, "I don't know what will happen next. We must continue to pray so that our heavenly Father can send us food."

The next morning at seven o'clock, a plane was seen circling over the town. It was big, and looked like a military plane. As it was about to land, though, Pastor Amosa saw the United Nations sign on it. He said, "We must be thankful. God has answered our prayers."

Lodu and the other children were very happy. They ran about shouting and jumping up and down. Kaku, who had been resting under a tree, got up as the noise grew louder and louder. She could not understand what was happening until Lodu ran to her and said, "A plane has brought some food."

Pastor Amosa decided to go to the church office in the town, to see when the food might be unloaded. At noon he returned. The children watched him get off his bicycle. His face was not happy.

"I'm sorry to tell you that the plane that came was not carrying any food," Pastor Amosa said in a trembling voice. "We can still feel happy though, because it has brought us medicines. Medicines that can cure many different types of diseases."

There was complete silence in the compound. Nobody sang or shouted. "What use is medicine if we starve to death?" they seemed to ask by their silence.

Lodu went to his mother and told her that there was no food. Staying at the church compound was not going to help them.

He couldn't help crying as he gave her this bad news, and she couldn't help crying either. She had lost her husband because of the war and her son was fatherless. She looked at him and tried to control herself. Lodu too tried to think what to do.

He once had heard his father talking about their home being at a certain place called Gumeiza. If only his mother could tell him how to get there! He did not wish to stay at the church compound. This was not the solution to their problem. Home was better.

"We should go to Gumeiza," he told his mother. "We'll find plenty of food there, and we won't hear the sound of guns."

"How are we going to get there?" Kaku asked, with her eyes full of tears. If they left the safety of the church compound, they could easily be killed, she thought.

"I know how we can get there," Lodu told his mother, desperately.

Lodu had seen people bringing firewood into the compound and selling it to others. Some of the boys had told him that many people had found their way into the countryside by pretending they were going to look for firewood. Lodu and his mother could get to Gumeiza if they used the same trick. Lodu remembered the axe they had brought from Muniki. This would help them with their plan.

Early the next morning Lodu and his mother went to Pastor Amosa's house. They found him sitting outside, writing in a book.

"What can I do for you?" he asked.

"Mother and I would like to go to look for some firewood," Lodu answered. "We haven't got any salt. If we sell the firewood we can get some money, and then we can buy some salt," Lodu explained, looking at the ground.

Pastor Amosa, who was used to such requests, said softly to Lodu and his mother, "Go and be careful. There are booby traps everywhere. You must go with a guide who will show you the safe path to follow."

Lodu tried to be brave. He and his mother went back to where they had left their little bundle. Kaku put this on her head and with Lodu leading the way, they left the church compound. They passed several villages, but there were no people living in them. When they reached a place called Rejaf, they stopped under a tree to rest.

As they sat there, Lodu heard some men talking. He went to find them, and discovered a big wide river with reeds growing on the banks. Three men were there, fishing.

"Can you help my mother and me across the river?" Lodu asked.

"We don't have a canoe," answered one of the men. "Why can't you swim? The river isn't deep."

Lodu went back to his mother, and brought her to the river bank. The brown water was flowing very fast and looked very deep. She felt afraid.

Lodu walked some distance down the river, hoping he would find a place to cross. Suddenly he saw a hippopotamus come to the surface of the river. He saw its large eyes, and brown skin with only a little hair on it. It breathed out water through its large nostrils. Then, not far from the hippo, Lodu saw something thin and black. He looked closer. When it moved, he realized it was a crocodile.

Lodu quickly ran to where his mother was sitting. Breathing heavily he said to her, "There are hippos and crocodiles in this river! I have seen them come to the surface. We can't cross it!"

His mother trembled, but told him to search in the other direction. He went up the river. There in the reeds he saw a canoe. Then he knew that the fishermen had lied. Lodu understood that the fishermen did not help anyone for free. But he and his mother had nothing to give them.

It was now very late in the afternoon. Lodu and his mother did not know what to do. Kaku was feeling tired, and decided they should rest. She untied her bundle, which was really a small sheet, and spread it out to sleep.

"Can you give us that cloth?" one of the fishermen asked. "We could make a sail with it."

"This is all we have to use as both a bag and a sheet,"

Kaku said.

"If you give it to us we will help you," the fisherman told her.

Kaku had no choice. She gave them the piece of cloth.

"Ahh, now we will help you to cross the river," said one of the fishermen. "We've got a canoe hidden in the reeds."

Lodu was overjoyed when he saw the fisherman come back, paddling the canoe. Lodu and mother got in, holding their few belongings, and were taken across the river.

Although it was dark, Kaku knew they must get away from the river. She did not trust the fishermen. "We must not spend the night here," she told her son. "We'll have to walk until we can walk no more. That's when we'll make a fire and try to rest."

The two walked for more than five hours in the night. Finally they came to a big tree. Kaku said they could stop. As Lodu slept his mother kept watch until morning. She heard lions roaring, but that did not frighten her. Hyenas and leopards made frightful noises, but Lodu did not hear them. He was tired and he slept soundly.

Kaku was tired too, but they had come this far and she was determined to get to Gumeiza. Her son believed they would live in peace there and have plenty to eat. She hoped so too.

Early the next morning, Lodu and his mother started walking again. They had no food with them, but on the way they found wild fruits. At about three in the afternoon, they could see white smoke rising from a village. An hour later they realized they had made it safely to Gumeiza at last. Lodu's uncles and aunts were very happy to see them, and gave them milk mixed with porridge made from millet.

In the days that followed, Lodu and his mother settled down. His uncles helped him build huts for himself and his mother. He and his mother began to dig a plot of land, to grow food for themselves. Lodu became very happy because he was safe among his people. There would be no more sounds of shooting, no more running away.

He thought about Pastor Amosa, and the people back at the church compound. He hoped that God had answered their prayers, that food had come, and that they would be able to return home safely too. Maybe he would see his friends again some day.

The Rev. Gordon Tikiba, from Southern Sudan, is trained as a teacher and worked with the Southern Ministry of Education in Juba, Sudan, for many years. Before joining the Sudan Literature Centre (located in Nairobi, Kenya) in 1989, he was the Director of Curriculum Development. He wrote this story in 1992 at a Writing for Children Workshop given by Phoebe Mugo at Daystar University College in Nairobi.

Thoko's Visit

Susan Randall

Liziwe works in a large house in Johannesburg. She lives in a room outside the house. She lives alone, but she has quite a number of visitors.

Today is Thursday, and she does not have to work this afternoon. She has just finished cleaning the kitchen. Soon she will tidy the rest of the house. But first, she sits down with a cup of tea.

It is quiet. Everyone else has left the house. There is only the sound of birds and the far-away noise of cars. Liziwe listens to the birds for a while. Then she gets up to turn on the radio.

She hears a squeak outside. Someone is opening the gate. Liziwe goes to the window and looks out.

A little figure dressed in black and white slips through the gate. Liziwe opens the kitchen door.

"Thoko!" says Liziwe.

"Auntie," the girl answers quietly. She closes the gate behind her.

"What brings you here?" Liziwe asks. "Is everything all right?"

"It is fine," says Thoko.

"But you are in your school clothes," Liziwe says. "Why aren't you at school?"

"Oh," says Thoko. She looks down at her black dress. "I

didn't feel like going to school today."

Liziwe feels a hot pain in her head. Then the pain moves to her chest.

"Come and have some tea." Liziwe holds the door wide for Thoko, and Thoko walks into the kitchen. Liziwe is careful not to close the door too hard. She tries to forget about the hot pain in her head and chest.

But Liziwe is angry, and the anger will not go away. She wants to shout. She wants to scold Thoko. She wants to make Thoko understand how important school is. Instead she turns on the radio and takes some cleaning things from the cupboard.

While Thoko is drinking her tea, Liziwe starts cleaning the rest of the house. She is glad to be out of the kitchen. She does not want to see Thoko sitting there in her school dress. She cleans quickly and angrily. She makes the beds with sharp movements.

"What will you do today, Auntie?"

Liziwe turns at the sound of Thoko's voice. Thoko is standing in the doorway with her cup in her hands. Thoko knows that Thursday is Liziwe's short day. That is why she is here, thinks Liziwe, and her anger fades a little. She is glad that Thoko has come to be with her and is not wandering on the streets.

"I am not sure yet," Liziwe answers. Then she asks, "How often do you miss school like this?"

Thoko looks down. She does not answer.

The anger comes back to Liziwe. She picks up her duster and sweeps the dust from a shelf. Then she picks up two cushions and hits them together hard. "Every day?" she asks suddenly. "Is it every day that you miss school?"

"It is not every day," Thoko answers.

"Is it every second day? Is it every third day? Or is it once a week that you miss school? Even once a week is too often, child. It is too often!"

"You don't understand," Thoko says.

10

Liziwe stops her work and looks at Thoko. Her eyes feel as though they are on fire. She wants this fire to burn Thoko, but Thoko is looking down again.

"I don't understand," Liziwe repeats quietly. "You think I don't understand." Then she speaks very loudly. "Now tell me, what is it I don't understand?"

Thoko's body moves as though she wants to walk away but cannot.

"Tell me!" Liziwe says.

"There are not enough books," says Thoko. "I have to share with three others. And sometimes the teachers don't come when they should. And we have to learn English and Afrikaans. Why can't we just learn our own language? The white children don't learn Zulu or Tswana or Sotho... Why must we learn theirs? And everything gets stolen. My pen was stolen yesterday."

"You must look after your pen better," Liziwe says. "Then it won't disappear. And tell me what's wrong with sharing your books? To share is better than nothing at all."

"But the white children don't have to share."

"In my days, we would have been happy to have one book among twenty of us!" says Liziwe. "And learning Afrikaans and English is good. The more languages you can speak, the better it will be. Then there is no end to what you can learn! It's not good to know only half of what is said around you. Why do you think you are so unlucky? Why must you think that you should have been a white child!"

Suddenly a tear rolls down Thoko's cheek. Liziwe sees it, but she is still angry.

"People like me," Liziwe says, "did not have as much as you have. We did not have proper school. But we did not feel sorry for ourselves. No! We worked hard. We did not say, 'Look at how much the white children have.' No! We said, 'How can we make our own lives better?' And now things are better! But it is not good enough for you! We have saved our children from much pain, but they say, 'It is not enough.' What is enough, child? When will you be happy? When will you see how much you have?"

Thoko is sobbing now. Her breaths are deep and loud. The tears are coming fast.

"Tell me we did not work for nothing," Liziwe says. "Tell me that you are glad about school."

"I'm sorry, Auntie," Thoko whispers through the tears.

Liziwe puts down all her cleaning things. She walks to where Thoko is standing and touches her arm. "I do not like to see you cry," she says. "But you see, things could be worse. I know there are problems at school. But you make things worse when you don't go to school."

"I did not know," Thoko cries. "Please don't be cross."

Liziwe looks at Thoko's unhappy face. Then she says, "If I tell you my story, I think you will understand."

❖

"When I was a girl," Liziwe begins, "my father was a farm-worker in Natal. Every year he made a contract with a white farmer. Then my family stayed on that farmer's land.

"Sometimes we stayed for two or three years on the same farm, if the farmer was good to us and the work was all right. One farmer was not good. He drank too much beer. He shouted at my father and the other workers. We moved to another farm very soon.

"When there was too little rain, there was not enough work. So we had to move again. I do not remember all the farms. There were so many.

"One day when I was about eight years old my father made a contract with a farmer called Mr. Botha. My father had six sons and two daughters to help with the farm-work. So it was easy for him to make a contract. Mr. Botha was pleased to have many children to help with the work. That is why farm-workers like my parents often had big families. At that time, we black children were called 'hands.'"

Liziwe stops talking, pulls some wool towards her, and starts knitting.

12

"Why were you called that?" Thoko asks.

"Because we used our hands to work," Liziwe answers. "Our hands were important. My father had eight hands. The six boys helped with the oxen and the cows. They also helped with the work on the land."

"And the girls?" asks Thoko.

"My sister and I helped my mother with her work in the farmhouse. But sometimes we also helped with the work on the land. We always had to wake up early.

"On Monday it was washing day and we went with our mother to the big farmhouse. My mother tied the dirty wash in a large bundle. She put the bundle on her head and carried it over the *veld* to the river. The bundle was very heavy.

"I carried a big tin bath and a sack of dried mealie-cobs. My sister carried another sack of mealie-cobs. She also carried a three-legged pot and some farm soap.

"At the river we all looked for dried sticks and grass to make a fire. The mealie-cobs were for the fire. We filled the pot with water and put it on the fire to boil. When it was hot we washed the clothes in the tin bath. We scrubbed them on the rocks to make them clean. We rinsed them in the river."

"That is hard work for a little girl," says Thoko.

"Yes," Liziwe says. She twists her wool and looks into Thoko's eyes. Then she goes on knitting.

"We spread the washing on the grass or we hung it on the fence. Then we waited for the sun to dry the clothes. When it was dry we carried everything back to the farmhouse. The next day my mother ironed the washing.

"On Fridays we also went to the farmhouse. On Fridays we cleaned the whole house. My mother swept the floors very clean. Then she got down on her hands and knees and put polish on the floors. She rubbed the floor till it shone. The polish also made the floors smell fresh.

"My sister and I moved the furniture so that my mother

could polish everywhere. We also dusted the furniture and put polish on it. We rubbed and rubbed until the furniture was shiny. I also liked the smell of that polish.

"We brushed the mats and the carpets with a stiff brush. The dust flew everywhere and made us sneeze! Then we cleaned the windows with newspaper and spirits. Sometimes the spirits made my hands burn. We rubbed the glass to make it clean and shiny. Our arms ached!

"There was so much cleaning to be done! In the kitchen we cleaned out the coal stove. It was old and black. Then we polished that too. We also polished all the milk buckets and milk cans. We scrubbed the cooking pots and polished the knives, forks and spoons."

"Before we went home we swept the verandas and the drive outside the house. The farmhouse was always very clean on Fridays. I think Mrs. Botha liked having visitors on the weekends because of our work.

"When I was ten years old," Liziwe says, "my mother and father sent me to live in the town with my aunt. I went to school in the town. There was no school on the farm. Many of the farm-workers' children did not go to school because there were not many farm schools at that time. And many farm-workers could not read or write, so they could not teach their children.

"I looked after my aunt's baby in the town, because my aunt was working. I took the baby to an old woman every morning. Then I ran to school. I was in a class that had about sixty children in it.

"The teacher was often very cross. She hit the children. She shouted at us. There were too many children in the class. The teacher had only been to school up to Standard Six, but the children were frightened of her."

"We did not learn very much, but I learned to read and write a little Zulu. I also learned a little math.

"After school each day I ran to fetch the baby from the old woman. I took it to my aunt's house. I looked after the baby in the afternoons until my aunt came from work. I liked my aunt. She was very nice.

"I went to school for only one year. So I did not learn very much. Then I had to go home to the farm to look after my mother's baby because she had to work."

"I was glad to be with my parents again. But I was sorry to leave the school. I liked learning to read and write. I wanted to learn more. But I knew I was lucky, because some of my brothers did not go to school at all."

"You know so much, Auntie," Thoko says. "I want to be like you!"

Liziwe laughs. She puts her knitting down and stands up. "It is late, child. You must catch a taxi back home now. I will make you one last cup of tea, and then you should be on your way. Your mother will be home soon and we don't want her to worry about where you are."

Liziwe gives Thoko her cup of tea. She asks, "Have you learned anything from my story?"

Thoko looks down. Her face is like that of a very small girl. "I have learned so much," she says quietly. "I have a lot to think about now. I am sorry that I did not feel like going to school this morning."

"You are young," Liziwe says. "I am glad you have seen how lucky you are. It is not too late."

"I have just had a good idea," Thoko says. "I am going to do something, and I think you will like it. I will tell you the next time I see you."

On Saturday, Thoko comes into the kitchen and closes the door. Liziwe is speaking with Mrs. Smith, the owner of the house.

"Hello, Mrs. Smith. Hello, Auntie." Thoko greets them politely. She looks at Liziwe and says, "I have brought something to show you." She holds out a piece of paper. "It is the thing I could not tell you. Do you remember?"

"I remember," Liziwe answers. "The day I told you my story, you said you were going to do something I would like."

Mrs. Smith cannot understand what Liziwe and Thoko are saying. They are speaking in their own language.

"I hope that is not a letter with bad news," Mrs. Smith says.

Thoko giggles. She puts her hand over her mouth.

"I do not think so," Liziwe tells Mrs. Smith. She starts reading what is on the paper. Then she says to Thoko, "Mrs. Smith is worried. Tell her what this is all about."

Thoko looks shy again. But she looks at Mrs. Smith and says, "I wrote this letter. It is to other children at schools in the townships."

"Oh?" says Mrs. Smith. "What does it say, Thoko?"

Thoko smiles and looks at the floor. Then she says, "Aunt Liziwe has told me her story, about how she did not go to school as a child. It made me see that I am lucky today, and I wanted to tell the other children."

Liziwe had finished reading Thoko's letter. "It is a nice letter," she says in English. "Why don't you show Mrs. Smith?"

"I would like to see it," Mrs. Smith says.

Thoko smiles a big smile. She looks at her feet.

"May I see it?" Mrs. Smith asks.

Thoko nods her head, and Liziwe gives the letter to Mrs. Smith. Mrs. Smith reads Thoko's letter aloud. This is what she reads:

> I am a twelve-year-old girl. I am in Standard Six in Soweto. I used to stay away from school whenever I felt like it. When my friends told me to miss school I did.
>
> My aunt did not go to school as a girl, and she told me her story. Now I have changed. Now I can see how important school is. I am not a child anymore and now I want to finish my education. I also want to get good marks

on my exams.

I am writing this letter to all the other school children in townships. What I want to say is this: Think carefully about what you are doing. Don't stay away from school just because someone tells you to. We need education. The problems at school can be worked out. If we have an education we will be able to work them out.

From Thoko

Mrs. Smith is silent. She is still looking at the letter in her hands. Then she says, "This is a good letter, Thoko. You must send it to the newspaper."

"I do not know how to do that," Thoko whispers.

Mrs. Smith puts down her handbag. She puts down her shopping list. Then she leaves the kitchen. Soon she comes back with a big book in her hands.

"This is the telephone book," she says. "We will find the address of the newspaper in here."

Mrs. Smith flips through the pages of the book. Then she gives Thoko a pencil and says, "Write this down."

On the top of her letter, Thoko writes the address that Mrs. Smith reads out. Mrs. Smith looks at it to see that it is right. Then she takes the pencil from Thoko. At the top of Thoko's letter she writes, "Dear Editor." She tells Thoko that the editor is the person in charge of the newspaper.

"Now you can post your letter," Mrs. Smith says, "and we will see what happens." She looks at her watch. "Oh dear, it is late," she says. "I must go, before the shops close." Mrs. Smith picks up her bag and her shopping list. Then she is gone.

Ten days go by. Then Thoko's letter is in the newspaper with some other letters. Mrs. Smith sees this and shows Liziwe.

17

Liziwe laughs when she sees Thoko's letter. She says, "Thoko told me she was going to do something I would like. She was right! I like seeing this letter in the newspaper!"

"If you had not told Thoko your story, she would not have done it," Mrs. Smith says. "It is you who has helped her so much."

Liziwe keeps the newspaper. The next time Thoko visits, Liziwe shows her the page where the letter is printed.

"I am proud of you, child," Liziwe says.

"Thank you, Auntie," Thoko answers shyly.

Then Thoko smiles a big smile.

Susan Randall, author of many poems and stories, was born in 1965 in Johannesburg. At 17, she won joint first prize in the South Africa Department of Education's national poetry competition. This story is based on the life of Selina Radebe, domestic worker to the Randall family for fifteen years. It is dedicated to her, "the real author of this story," and to Susan's mother, Isobel Randall, for encouraging her to write it.

The Red Kitenge

Rachel Mhimili

"Pendo! Come over here, I want to tell you a secret."
Rehema took her friend's hand and led her to the shade of
the school *shamba*. They crouched between the dry maize
stalks so none of their friends could see them.

"Pendo, do you know our village shopkeeper?"

"Yes, I think so. The tall man with the scar on his
cheek?" Rehema answered.

"Yes, that's him. He's my uncle. The people at the
warehouse in town have promised to give him a bale of
kitenge material next week. Pendo, he says it's the best
kitenge material we've ever had in our village. It's blue, the
color of the sky in the dry season, with a pattern of white
birds on it. My mother says she will buy me one. What
about you? Will you get one too so that we can dress alike?"
Rehema was excited just thinking about it.

Pendo didn't reply. Slowly she got up, and walked to the
far corner of the shamba. "A crisp, shiny kitenge," Pendo
thought. "I've never had a new kitenge." A tear rolled down
her cheek. She was so unhappy.

Pendo was in Standard Five at the village primary
school. She liked it very much and tried hard in her lessons.
Her uncle hadn't wanted her to go to school. He wanted her
to stay at home and look after his children. But one day a
visitor came to their house. He explained that it was the law

19

in Tanzania for children of eight years and above to be in school. So reluctantly he had sent her.

"If only my clothes were nice like those of my friends," Pendo said to herself. Her only kitenge and her school uniform were full of holes and shabby. She had no shoes. She tried really hard to wash her clothes clean, but they were worn out. They had already been worn by other girls before being passed on to her.

Pendo wiped her eyes and began to walk back to her classroom. Perhaps she could find a way of getting enough money to buy one of those blue *vitenge*.

She rushed home from school that day. She wanted to talk to her aunt when her uncle wasn't around.

"Auntie, why won't Uncle buy me any new clothes like he buys your children? Why is he always angry with me?"

Her aunt sighed. She wished her husband would treat Pendo better instead of always being unkind and angry.

"If only I was stronger," she thought to herself, "I would do most of the housework. Pendo is so young." But she did not have good health after bearing many children. She couldn't do the heavy work around the house.

"Uncle wasn't happy when we brought you here. Do you remember that time? You were still quite a small girl," she said.

"I can remember a long, dusty journey on a bus with Uncle. He hardly spoke to me the whole way. When we arrived and came into this house, I was surrounded by lots of children whom I didn't know!" Now Pendo could laugh about it but at the time it was frightening.

"Do you know why we brought you to live here?" Auntie asked her quietly.

"My mother died, didn't she?" Pendo could remember just a little of what happened. One day her mother had become very ill. She was in great pain. Pendo was still small so she couldn't help her. As her mother cried in pain, Pendo also cried. Though she cried loudly no one came. All the villagers were out working in their shambas. When they returned at sunset, some heard the crying and came to see what was wrong.

"It was very hot and the women made a lot of noise. One picked me up and took me to her house. I never saw my mother again after that."

"Yes, we heard the women found you very tired and dirty, still crying and sitting near where your mother lay. She had died before the women got there. She'd been so upset by what happened to your father that when she got ill, she had no strength to fight it."

"What did happen to my father?" That was one question no one ever answered. She'd asked her aunt many times but she would never tell her. It was the same now.

"Go and start the fire. You know how angry your uncle gets if supper isn't on the table when he returns."

The next day at school Pendo was again thinking, "How can I get some money for the blue kitenge?"

It was an arithmetic lesson. She must work hard.

"How many times does six go into forty-two?" asked the teacher. Pendo's hand shot up.

"Yes, Pendo?"

"Seven times, teacher."

"That's correct. And how many times does eight go into sixty-four?...seven into forty-two...?" Teacher continued to ask many questions. Almost every time Pendo's was the first hand to go up.

The lesson that followed was science. Teacher asked, "What plants grow well in areas with a lot of rain?"

The pupils replied, "Wheat, pineapples, tea..."

"And here where there's not much rain, what grows well?" Many hands went up.

"Millet, sorghum, groundnuts, grapes..." they answered.

Pendo had an idea. "Groundnuts! I could plant some groundnuts. That would be a way of getting enough money for the kitenge."

Pendo always got up early to go into the bush to cut firewood. Then she would return, and make tea for all the family, and help wash the little children before she went to school. Now she got up even earlier in the mornings. Before going to cut firewood, she went to a small corner of her uncle's shamba. She cultivated it well and spread manure on the soil. She planted the groundnuts and before long they sprouted.

A week later, when Pendo went into the church for Sunday school, she saw the children crowding around someone. It was Rehema, wearing a new kitenge–a blue kitenge with a white bird pattern. Pendo turned away and went to sit in a corner.

"Rehema is lucky, but what about me?" she thought. "Does Jesus really love me like they say?" That day Pendo found it difficult to keep her mind on what their teacher was saying. She was upset. But suddenly something the teacher was saying got through to her.

"You can talk to Jesus just like you talk to your best friend. In fact it's better! When you tell your best friend your problems, she can't often help you, but Jesus can. He will always help if you ask him."

Pendo decided to tell Jesus her problems. On those early morning walks to get firewood she began talking with him as though he was right beside her. She began to feel less lonely. She began to understand that there was someone who loved her and who knew her problems.

"God is love, he loves me," Pendo sang joyfully as she weeded her shamba. She too had a secret now.

It wasn't too long before the groundnuts were ready for harvesting. She spread the groundnuts in the sun. When they were quite dry she put them in a *debe* and was surprised that they filled it right to the top.

On Saturday she put the debe on her head and set off for the market. She was so pleased when she sold them for two hundred shillings. She gave twenty shillings to her aunt. The remaining one hundred and eighty she kept in a safe place for when the shop got more kitenge material. She knew it wouldn't be as nice as the blue with the white bird pattern but she didn't mind.

"You're a good girl," her auntie said, remembering how hard Pendo worked without complaining. Pendo went to bed, full of hope.

That night the whole household was woken by a great screeching and squealing. Pendo's uncle opened the shutters and shone his torch across the courtyard to the hen house. Suddenly he turned and ran back to the bedroom. He returned a few seconds later, holding his shotgun in one hand and fumbling as he tried to load the bullets into it.

"Honey badger," he muttered as he went to the window. The children all huddled together in a corner. They knew just how dangerous honey badgers were. With their long, curved claws they could tear a person to bits. That was why Uncle wasn't going out into the courtyard but trying to aim at the animal in the dark. He saw two eyes gleaming.

Crack! A shot rang out. The children's hearts jumped. Outside it became quiet.

"Go back to bed, all of you," Uncle shouted as he undid the latch on the door. Pendo could hear him moving around outside and talking under his breath.

"Pendo!" he shouted. Pendo lay rigid on her goat skin. His voice sounded so angry. "Pendo, come here!" Pendo was shaking all over. Her uncle stood in the doorway holding a headless chicken. Blood was running down his arm.

"Eight dead chickens including the cock, all because you didn't lock the door of the hen house last night!" He dropped the hen, picked up a stick and began to beat Pendo.

"You're a useless, good-for-nothing girl." Almost under his breath, he added, "child of a murderer."

Pendo staggered back to the bedroom. She was blinded

by tears and pain. Some of the children moved over to make room for her on the mattress. She was too bruised to lie on the floor. She sobbed and sobbed. Little Sara moved over and put her arms around her. Filipo was crying too. He had heard what his father said. It was his job to lock up the hens, not Pendo's. He knew she did not deserve that beating.

As the sun rose Pendo's aunt came into their room. She had brought a bowl of water and a cloth. She began to bathe Pendo's head, arms and back. Pendo sobbed quietly.

"Auntie, what did Uncle mean when he said 'child of a murderer'?"

There were tears in her aunt's eyes too. "Uncle was very cruel to you last night Pendo, not only with the beating, but also with his words."

"But what did he mean? Was he talking about my father?" Pendo had once been told that her father was in prison but no one had ever told her anything more.

"Yes, he was, Pendo. But your father wasn't a murderer. He killed someone by accident."

"Tell me about it, Auntie. I'm not a little girl anymore. I can understand."

"When you were very little you lived with your mother and father a long way away in a village called Hanene. One night there was an argument. Some of the men of the village were drunk. They got very angry and began to fight. Like most men, your father carried a knife in his belt. Another man grabbed it from its leather case. He wanted to use it in the fight. Your father saw the danger and snatched it back. Just at that moment a man near your father received a blow from behind. He fell onto the knife. When they turned him over, he was dead, with your father's knife in his chest."

There was a long silence. Pendo said, "Poor father...but didn't they know it was an accident?"

"Yes, most people did. But they were scared. You see, the one who hit the man who fell on the knife and died was

24

the brother of the village chairman. Because of this, people were afraid to speak the truth when the case came up. So your father was put in prison.

"I went to see him once just after your mother died. I told him what had happened and promised that Uncle and I would look after you. I hadn't been married very long and Filipo was just a baby. I didn't realize how your uncle would be hard on you. He never let me go and see your father again, even though he's my brother."

She took Pendo's hand and squeezed it lovingly as she looked into her sad eyes.

"You lie there today, Pendo. You won't be able to go to school for a day or two. Your face and arm are swollen and your back is badly bruised. I'll do my best to keep Uncle away from you. He went off to the meat market early this morning so I don't think he'll be back until night."

She sent Filipo off to the dispensary to get some aspirins. When he came back, she made Pendo take two. The pain eased a bit. She slept most of the day, but it was another three days before she was able to return to school.

One evening while she was cooking supper, she heard the sound of a child running towards the house. She raised her head. It was Rehema.

"I have good news, Pendo! Tomorrow there will be new vitenge at the shop. Get up early and go to the shop with your money."

Rehema knew how Pendo had saved the money from her groundnuts. Pendo was very happy. She began to think how she could arrange her work so that she could still be at the shop early. Tomorrow was Saturday, so there would be no school. She went on cooking the spinach and *ugali*, but all her thoughts were about vitenge! She imagined different colors and patterns and tried to picture herself in them. When the food was ready she put some on the table for her uncle and returned to the kitchen to eat hers with the other children.

"Pendo, come here," her uncle called sharply.

"Tomorrow you will come with me to Mkweka, to help my friend harvest his maize. We will buy some for ourselves and return with it in the evening."

Pendo felt like bursting into tears. "What can I do?" she thought. "I can't say to my uncle, 'I can't go with you, I'm going to get a kitenge tomorrow.' He'll beat me again if I say that!"

"Be ready early," her uncle ordered. "We'll leave here at five."

She held back her tears and with a voice that could hardly be heard said, "Yes, Uncle, I'll be ready."

She went back to the kitchen and washed the pots but her eyes were filled with tears. Sleep was a long time coming that night.

"Lord Jesus, you love me, I know. Why do things always seem to go badly for me?" She felt sad. Her thoughts were confused.

Early the next morning she climbed on the back of her uncle's bicycle. They went to harvest the maize of her uncle's friend. Others were there to help. The sun was hot but they worked hard. By three in the afternoon they had finished. They strapped one sack of maize on the bicycle and began to walk home. They got back just before sunset.

Ignoring her tiredness, Pendo ran to get the money she'd hidden in the bedroom. She ran as fast as she could to the village shop. It was still open. Pendo was breathless with running and excitement.

"I'd like a kitenge. Look, here's the money!"

The shopkeeper gazed at her. He saw her eyes were shining. He knew the home in which Pendo lived. She wouldn't have money of her own. Pendo guessed his thoughts.

"I wanted a new kitenge so much. I've never had any new clothes ever. So I made my own little shamba and grew groundnuts. I sold a whole debe and that's how I got the money for a kitenge." The shopkeeper felt sorry but he had to tell her.

"It's true we did have vitenge today, but we've sold them already. Why didn't you come earlier?"

Pendo didn't wait to reply. She ran and flung herself on the ground under a tree and cried and cried. But it was getting dark. She knew she must go home and cook the evening meal.

While she was eating in the kitchen with the other children, someone knocked at the front door. She heard her uncle letting a visitor in, then the sound of talking. After a while she was called.

"Pendo, come here."

"Perhaps there's not enough food for the visitor and they want me to cook some more," thought Pendo. She went into the living room. Near her uncle sat a thin, kind-looking man. She greeted him politely in the customary way. He was gazing at her. No one said anything.

Pendo felt very uneasy. She did not know what to do. She looked at her uncle, expecting him to tell her what he wanted. But he was silent. The visitor was still looking at her. She looked at her aunt. There was a soft smile on her face, but she didn't say anything either.

"What do they want?" she thought, and felt herself trembling. She saw on the table, in front of the visitor, a small parcel. Her eyes darted away again but the visitor had noticed.

"Take it," he said. She couldn't believe her ears, and hesitated.

"Take it and open it," said the visitor. Pendo went slowly to the table and took the parcel. She began to open it but her trembling made it difficult.

"Why aren't they saying anything?" she was still wondering. "And who is the visitor?" She looked at the parcel more closely and pulled at the tape. This time the paper came off. She gasped. A kitenge, a beautiful new kitenge. She spread it out. It was red with a black and white pattern of stars. This was the nicest kitenge she'd ever, ever seen. Pendo was amazed. Still trembling, she turned her eyes to the visitor once more.

"It's for you, Pendo. I'm your father."

Pendo had been so surprised when she saw the kitenge, but now she just gaped. She didn't know what to do.

The visitor stood up, came towards her and hugged her. For Pendo it was as though something snapped inside her. She began to sob. She couldn't remember ever having been hugged before. This time her tears were not of sadness but of great joy. Her father held her tight. His eyes were not dry either.

Later, as they sat drinking the tea which her aunt made for them, her father began to talk. He explained that he had finished his time in prison. While there he had been taught the trade of carpentry. He did well. It seemed he had a gift for making things with wood. By selling them he had made enough money to start a small workshop in his village. He had built a little house, too.

"Now I've come to take you home to live with me again, Pendo."

The next day was Sunday. Pendo went to church with her father. She wore her new, crisp, red kitenge. On that long-awaited day it was not the red kitenge that she was proud of, however. It was her father, sitting beside her.

Rachel Mhimili is the pen name of the Tanzanian author. She wrote the story in 1984 at a workshop organized by several church publishing houses in Africa and funded by the World Association for Christian Communication. Phoebe Mugo was the coordinator of the project. This story was published in KiSwahili as *Kitenge Chekundu*. The English version appears now for the first time.

Pamela Hasegawa

Mother and son heading for home in Gamogofa Province, Ethiopia

❖

David P. Young

Baby washing time in Malawi

Beverly Conley

Church procession during Carnival time on Brava, Cape Verde

❖

Muslim girl in a refugee camp at Gabahare, Somalia

Richard Lord

Playtime for kindergartners in Kemba, Ethiopia

❖

Soccer team in Kitwe, Zambia, Africa's "copper belt"

Beverly Conley

*Brother and sister
gathering firewood on
the Cape Verde island
of Fogo*

❖

Pamela Hasegawa

Young boy herding cattle in the hills of southern Ethiopia

A Match Against Juju

James Ebo Whyte

Ekow woke up with a start. His heart was beating fast. He rubbed his eyes. He looked around him. He looked at the walls. He saw the furniture moved to one corner. He sighed with relief.

"It was only a dream," he thought, "a very bad dream."

He quickly rolled up his sleeping mat and pulled the furniture back into place. Then he went for a broom and started sweeping. The family's sitting room became Ekow's bedroom at night.

He heard footsteps.

"Good morning, father," Ekow said.

"Good morning, my son," his father said. "How are you this morning?"

"Fine, thank you."

His father took a newspaper from the center table and turned to go.

"Dad, have I told you that we are playing the Colts Knockout Finals today?"

"Yes. You said your team would play for the cup this afternoon."

"It is going to be a tough match."

"I expect so," his father said. "I met Mr. Togbe, the team manager of Agoromma yesterday. He said they are going all out for today's match, so be ready. He surprised me by saying that if he had to kill before his team could win the cup, he was prepared to do so!"

"That man is capable of anything. He believes so much in *juju*."

"Juju in a Colts team?" Ekow's father was surprised. "That is terrible. Does your team manager also believe in juju?"

"Mr. Amfoh doesn't. He says God is greater than any juju. So he makes us train hard and pray. We begin and end each match and even each training with a prayer. He makes every Sankofa player learn a Bible verse by heart every week."

"That's good. Have you learned the verse for this week?"

"Yes, Romans chapter 8, verse 31. 'If God is for us, who can be against us?'"

"That's a good verse. If God is for us, no one, no juju, nothing at all can be against us. Make sure you don't ever forget that verse."

"I won't," Ekow promised. "Dad, will you come to watch the match?"

"Yes. I am coming with a few friends."

Ekow was happy his father would be on the field to watch the finals. "I shall make Father proud today. I shall play my best," Ekow thought.

Ekow hurried with his duties, ate his breakfast quickly and left to join his teammates at Mr. Amfoh's house.

As Ekow turned a corner near his house, two boys stood in his way. They were bigger than him, and were holding big sticks. Ekow saw Agoromma badges on their shirts. He moved to the right to pass by them. They moved to block him. He turned to the left. They quickly blocked his way.

Ekow knew they wanted to pick a fight with him. Then they would hurt him so he could not play that afternoon.

"Please, let me pass," Ekow said. They ignored him.

Ekow turned to go back. He found two others standing behind him. They also wore Agoromma badges. He turned round again to face the first two. He did not know what to do now. If he tried to use force, it would be four boys against him. If he ran, they could trip him with their sticks.

Ekow gave up. He began to pray silently.

Just then, he saw the eyes of one of the boys open wide. The boy whistled. The other two boys looked scared. They walked away in different directions. Ekow turned quickly, and saw a policeman coming down the road.

"Thank God," Ekow sighed with relief. He continued walking to Mr. Amfoh's house.

When Ekow got there, most of his teammates had arrived.

"Bad news!" they greeted him. "Mr. Kusi is the referee."

"Oh no!" Ekow groaned. "Then we have two teams to beat this afternoon."

"Two teams?" his teammates asked.

"Yes," Ekow said. "Mr. Kusi is a whole team by himself."

His friends laughed but Ekow did not. He was serious. Mr. Kusi could make it impossible for Sankofa to win.

"I don't know why he hates us so much," he said.

"I know," said Kobina, the captain and center half for Sankofa. "Did you know that the team we beat in the first round of the knockout was Kusi's team?"

Ekow shook his head.

"It was," Kobina continued. "He was so angry after the match that he broke up the team that very day. And he has not forgiven us since."

Ekow turned to the team manager. "Mr. Amfoh, can't we do something to change the referee?" he asked.

"The last time he refereed our match," Mr. Amfoh said, "he sent Seidu off the field without any real cause. I complained after the match, but because we won that match with ten players, the officials did not take it seriously.

Now, I shall raise it again. I hope they will listen and give us a new referee."

Ekow and his mates cheered.

"Don't be too hopeful about this," Mr. Amfoh said. "They might refuse to change him."

Ekow felt sad. Mr. Amfoh might have noticed, for he quickly added, "But Mr. Kusi or no Mr. Kusi, we are going to win the cup!"

Ekow and the others cheered loudly. "We shall overcome," they sang, "we shall overcome today. Deep in our hearts we do believe, we shall overcome today." They clapped their hands and danced.

Just then someone told Ekow, "Kweku is calling you outside."

Kweku was Ekow's best friend. Ekow ran out to see him. When he got close and looked at Kweku's face he knew something was very wrong. Kweku's eyes were full of fear. He was shivering.

"Ekow," he said in a low voice, "you must not play today."

"Why?"

"Agoromma have gone for a juju to kill anyone who scores a goal against them. The scorer will die on the spot. And who scores goals for Sankofa? You."

Ekow broke into a sweat. He remembered his dream. "No, I must forget it," he thought.

"I didn't want to believe it when I heard it," Kweku was saying. "But when I found out that the Agoromma team spent the night at the burial ground, I knew there might be something in it."

"Agoromma slept at the cemetery?" Ekow's voice was low. He remembered what his father had heard Mr. Togbe saying—that he was prepared to kill to win the match!

His dream now came to his mind again. He had dreamed of fierce dogs chasing him. He could not dodge them. He had woken up just as they caught up with him.

36

Ekow shivered. He did not want to die. But could he stay out of the match today?

He thought of his father who would be there with his friends to watch it. He thought of his teammates. If he did not play, they would be discouraged. Then he thought of Mr. Amfoh. He knew Mr. Amfoh liked him and expected him to help Sankofa to win. He did not want to let him down.

Ekow knew what Mr. Amfoh would say if he told him about the juju. He would say juju had no effect on anyone who believed in God and tried to please God in everything.

"Ekow," Kweku asked, "what are you going to do?"

"I don't know," Ekow replied.

"Ekow!" Mr. Amfoh called from the house. "Time for lunch. You may come along with your friend."

As Ekow and Kweku entered, Ekow said, "Don't tell anyone else."

At the table, Ekow could not eat his food. When he held his fork and knife, his hands shook. He nearly spilled his water. His teammates laughed at him.

"Relax," Mr. Amfoh said. "Forget about the cup. Just make up your mind to play your best."

After lunch, Mr. Amfoh made them lie down to relax. But Ekow could not lie still. A little while later, Mr. Amfoh called all the players together.

"This is our great day," he said. "Let's make the most of it. And let's trust God to help us do our best and to protect us and Agoromma from any harm."

Mr. Amfoh always asked his boys to pray for those they were playing against. "They are not our enemies but our friends," he often said.

He gave them their blue jerseys.

"I know what I'll do," Ekow thought as he put on his jersey. "I'll play but refuse to score. I'll give all the chances to Seidu."

Seidu played inside left. He was the only other Sankofa

forward player who could score goals. The others were only good at creating chances for Seidu or Ekow to score.

It occurred to Ekow that he had not seen Seidu yet.

"Have you seen Seidu?" he asked Kweku.

"Seidu is hiding," Kweku whispered. "He also has heard of the juju."

Ekow was nervous. He heard a lorry blow its horn. It was the lorry to take the team to the field. The others cheered and ran outside. But Ekow was hesitant. He entered the lorry slowly. There were many boys surrounding it. They were cheering the team.

"Up Sankofa! Up Sankofa! Down Agoromma! Down Agoromma!" some chanted. "Champions! Champions!" others shouted. As the lorry moved, the boys ran after it.

It was a bright afternoon. From a distance, Ekow could only see a sea of heads around the field.

The crowd cheered as Sankofa approached the field. The players marched to the center, formed a circle in the middle of the field, and prayed. After the prayer, the Sankofa boys spread out to warm up. Ekow wished that someone would hurt him in the very first minute.

On one side of the field, just beyond the center line, was a big table covered with a white cloth. On it was the cup. It shone in the sun. Behind the table sat the officials. One seat was empty. It was reserved for the chief of the town, who would present the cup. Ekow gazed at the cup for a long time. Then he saw Mr. Amfoh talking to the officials and went down to listen.

"If you don't change him, I shall call my boys off the field," Mr. Amfoh was saying. "We have already made a complaint about him. You have not looked into the case yet. So we can't be sure he'll be fair to us now."

The officials talked among themselves. "We don't want anything to spoil today's match because the chief will be here."

"Go. We'll change him," one of them said.

Ekow heard the decision but did not know whether to be happy or sad. Mr. Kusi would have made it difficult for him to score a goal. Mr. Kusi could even have sent him off the field.

Ekow heard drums beating. Every eye turned to look in the direction of the sound. The chief was arriving, dressed in a rich *kente* cloth and wearing a big golden chain around his neck. He walked with slow, steady steps. His attendant held an umbrella over his head. The chief walked onto the field and the drumming stopped. All eyes turned in the opposite direction where loud cheers and chanting could be heard.

"Agoromma! Agoromma!"

Agoromma entered the field, wearing red jerseys. They scattered all over the field, running here and there, warming up.

The new referee walked smartly onto the field followed by two linesmen.

The two teams lined up. The chief shook hands with each player as he was introduced by his captain. The chief wished all of them well. After this there was the toss of the coin. Agoromma won. Kofi, captain for Agoromma, chose the end that had the sun behind the post. He knew the glare of the sun would make it difficult for Sankofa to score. The Agoromma supporters moved behind that goal post. Sankofa supporters also moved to their half of the field.

Sankofa kicked off.

Midway in the first half, a high pass found Ekow just in front of Agoromma's penalty box. He jumped, stopped the ball with his chest and shot at the goal.

The spectators yelled, "Goal!"

Ekow felt his heart jump in alarm. He had forgotten his decision and had shot at the goal out of habit. Amadu, Agoromma's goalkeeper, dived as the crowd yelled and saved the ball. The spectators clapped. Ekow sighed with relief.

"I'll have to be careful from now on," he thought.

The game continued. Soon Ekow had another chance to score. He had only Addo, the Agoromma center half, to pass. Ekow wished Addo would take the ball from him quickly. But to Ekow's dismay, Addo tripped and fell. Ekow was left alone. The spectators cheered him on. He hesitated. The spectators became impatient.

"Go!" they shouted. Ekow ran half-heartedly towards the goal. He wanted the Agoromma boys to catch up. But they had given up.

"If I kick it, I might beat the goalkeeper," Ekow thought. "I know what to do, I'll force him to catch it. I'll go straight to him."

Ekow got closer to the penalty area. He saw Amadu run out to meet him."

"Shoot!" the spectators yelled.

Ekow did not shoot. He pushed the ball a bit too far from him. This gave Amadu an advantage. He quickly dived for the ball. Ekow made no attempt to tackle him. He happily jumped over Amadu.

The spectators booed. "Shame!"

"Have you taken a bribe?" some asked. "He must be changed!" others said.

Ekow wished Mr. Amfoh would heed this last comment.

At half-time, Kweku pulled Ekow aside. "You nearly scored a goal," he said. His voice showed that he was afraid for his friend. Ekow did not say anything. He walked away.

He sat away from his teammates, feeling guilty for wasting their chances. But his teammates were not angry with him.

Ekow looked towards the spectators. He spotted his father. His father was looking at him. Ekow looked away quickly. He wanted his father to be proud of him, but he knew he was not playing his best.

Ekow could not bring himself to look at Mr. Amfoh. Tears filled his eyes but he held them back. "I don't want to let them down," he said to himself. "But then, there's the juju."

Mr. Amfoh served the team with an orange drink.

"My boys," he said, "let's go all out in the second half. Let's make our God, our families and our friends proud of us."

The whistle blew. As Ekow stood to go to his position, he felt an arm around his shoulders. He looked up. Mr. Amfoh was smiling at him.

"Back up," he said softly. "I'll be praying for you."

"I'll be praying for you," Ekow's mind repeated. "Then I don't have to fear anything. God will take care of me."

"But what if God doesn't?" The thought stole into his mind.

For most of the second half, Ekow used every trick he could think of to avoid scoring. He held on to the ball for too long. When he found an opponent standing before him in the penalty area, he kicked the ball against him. This, he thought, would look as if he wanted to score but the opponent had blocked the ball.

Then the Agoromma captain, Kofi, scored a beautiful goal for his side. Agoromma's supporters flooded the field. They carried Kofi high. Some shouted at the top of their voices. Others danced as they chanted.

"Agoromma! Champions! Agoromma! Champions!"

With ten minutes more to go Sankofa was still a goal down.

Ekow had a pass in Agoromma's half of the field. He ran forward with it, expecting the opponents to tackle him, but they fell back. Soon he found himself in the penalty area. Addo ran towards him. Ekow quickly kicked the ball at him. It hit his hands. The referee blew his whistle. He pointed to the penalty spot.

"Oh no!" Ekow cried in despair. He sank to the ground.

But his teammates were very happy. They lifted him up.

"That was a beautiful trick," they told him. "You'll have

to take it. You are our penalty expert."

Ekow stared at his friends. He was speechless. He wanted to tell them to find someone else to take the penalty kick. But words escaped him. He felt as if he were dreaming. He saw people jumping and moving all around him. But he could not move.

Amadu, the Agoromma goalkeeper, ran to him.

"If you score, you'll die," he whispered.

Then the words of the Bible passage came back to Ekow. "If God is for us, who can be against us?"

Ekow smiled. He repeated the verse. He remembered his father's comments. "If God is for us, no one, no juju, nothing at all can be against us."

The referee's whistle blew for the penalty to be taken. Ekow ran slowly to the ball. He pointed to Amadu's left and pretended he was going to kick in that direction, then twisted and shot to the right.

Amadu dove to the left. The ball went past him and hit the net.

"Goal!" the spectators shouted.

Ekow's heart jumped. He looked at himself and was surprised to find he was still standing. He felt a lot of hands touch him and lift him up. Some spectators were carrying him. Others were dancing.

"I am still alive!" Ekow thought. I did not die!"

Finally, they put him down. He looked at his hands and feet. He jumped up and down to make sure he was whole.

"Ekow!" he heard someone call.

He turned. It was Kweku. His eyes were wide and he was trembling.

Ekow held his friend by the shoulders and shook him hard. "Kweku," he said, "I did not die. And I won't die."

It took a long time for the referee to clear the field of happy spectators.

Agoromma kicked off. Full of confidence, Ekow ran to tackle. He got the ball. He quickly ran past two opponents.

He swerved to the right, causing Addo to run past him. He saw Amadu running towards him. He quickly kicked the ball past Amadu. The ball went into the net.

"Goal!" the spectators yelled again.

Now it was two goals to one in favor of Sankofa. Just after the kickoff, the referee looked at his watch.

"Prrrr!" the whistle blew. The game was over.

Many of the spectators ran to Ekow. They carried him all over the field. Some people gave him money. When they put him down, he ran to join his team for the closing ceremony. He gave all the money the spectators had given him to Kobina, the captain.

Mr. Amfoh walked to Ekow. "You did not die, did you?" he said.

Ekow looked at him in surprise. "You knew about the juju, then?" Ekow asked.

"Yes," Mr. Amfoh replied. "I wanted to see if all that we'd learned together would help you."

"I learned a lesson on the field today that I'll never forget," Ekow said. "For me, this was a match against juju and I've won it."

James Ebo Whyte of Ghana wrote this story about soccer and witchcraft at a 1984 workshop coordinated by Phoebe Mugo on behalf of several Christian publishers in Africa. It was published in KiSwahili as *Uchawi Katika Mchezo wa Mpira*, and appears now in English for the first time.

Kalulu's Cave

Peter Njoroge Mwaura

"Police reports say Benny 'Bad' Bunde, a dangerous criminal, escaped from prison two days ago."

Otieno and Sebastian strained to hear the rest. The radio announcer continued in his clipped accent.

"Bunde, a notorious drug dealer, was serving a five-year jail term. The Police Commissioner has offered a reward of 20,000 Kenya shillings to anyone with information leading to his arrest. And now the weather forecast..."

"Hey, Sebastian, think of all the things we could buy with such a lot of money. Let's look for him!" Otieno exclaimed to his older brother.

"You must be joking. Such men are killers," answered Sebastian. "And anyway, you are scared of learning how to swim, how can you even think — ?" His voice trailed off.

"Well, think of the adventure we'd have!" Otieno said.

In the other room, their mother listened to them. She was surprised. Otieno usually was such a careful lad, unlike Sebastian, her first-born son. At fourteen Sebastian was proud.

"Hey, you two! Please go to the river to fetch me water. I am so tired after working on the *shamba*," their mother called out.

Otieno readied himself, and carried a torch in case they

44

were late. But Sebastian did not want to go with him. He preferred to go alone or not at all.

"Sebastian!" mother called out again. "Why don't you go with your brother?"

"He's always getting me into trouble," he complained.

Otieno bit his lips and lowered his eyes. "Why did his brother always say bad things about him?" he wondered, gritting his teeth.

The two boys made their way down to the river. Even though it was a Saturday, only a few people were around. Most were working in their shambas, as this was the rainy season.

"Could you teach me how to swim, before we draw the water?" Otieno asked, lowering the big plastic container.

Sebastian shrugged. "If you say so." He was an expert swimmer. For some time now, he had been trying to instruct Otieno, but with little success. They removed their clothes and walked into the water.

"Lift your legs and stretch your hands forward," Sebastian instructed.

Otieno tried. As soon as he lifted his feet, he staggered and gulped a mouthful of the murky water. He tried again.

"Try harder," complained Sebastian. "When I was your age, I could swim across the river and back in ten minutes."

"What Sebastian said is true, but he has forgotten something," Otieno thought sadly to himself, as he tried to tread water. "Uncle Kairu was so patient and kind when he taught Sebastian."

Soon, they gave up. "Why don't we visit Kalulu's cave?" Sebastian suggested. Otieno knew his brother was bored.

"Okay. But let's not stay for long." They put on their clothes and headed for the cave.

Now Kalulu's cave was really an odd place. Nobody seemed to know the truth about it. Otieno had once asked his grandfather about it.

"My child, I have lived many, many years," the old man

had said. Then he answered with a question. "Can someone put his finger in a lion's mouth and expect to live?"

Otieno reminded Sebastian of that conversation.

"Grandfather is too old!" Sebastian answered scornfully.

But as they climbed the stony hill next to the cave, Sebastian's heart was racing. His hair felt stiff and angry knots knitted his stomach. Otieno noticed.

"Are you scared?" he asked his brother.

"Who, me? Scared?" Sebastian tried to laugh it off. "I will go in first, then you'll follow."

They pushed themselves through the narrow entrance of the cave. The uneven ground was sandy and damp in some places. The cave was shaped like a broken circle, and it was dark. Very dark.

"Do you think we should be doing this?" Otieno asked Sebastian as he held his breath.

"Aw, shut up! I shouldn't have brought you. You're such a chicken," hissed cruel Sebastian.

"At least use my torch then. It's too dark to see anything," the younger boy replied.

"What on earth is this?" Sebastian exclaimed, frozen.

Otieno froze too in surprise. In the narrow beam of light, they saw a stack of jute bags. They hurried over.

"It must be some treasure!" said Sebastian.

Before Otieno could reply, his nose twitched once, then twice as he sneezed a loud "Achoo!"

"It must be onions," Otieno thought, recalling how his eyes and nose watered whenever he was peeling onions.

Sebastian's hands tugged furiously as he untied the top sack. The sisal ropes loosened quickly.

"Gosh, we're in trouble!" he said. In his hands he held some dry, harmless looking herbs.

Otieno was puzzled. "Trouble? Is this some kind of poison?" he asked.

"This is a drug. It's called *bhang* or marijuana or even *bomb*. Some kids smoke it in school. But don't tell mum a word about it."

Something clicked in Otieno's mind. That news item on the radio—it must be connected to all this! The police had to be informed.

"Sebastian," he whispered, "let's get out of here. This must be Bad Bunde's hideout."

Sebastian had forgotten all about that. "Let's run," he agreed.

Just as they neared the entrance to the cave, they heard heavy footsteps. Sebastian quickly flicked his light off. Both boys tensed motionless on the sandy ground.

"It's a man," Otieno whispered. "What do we do now?"

"Shh," Sebastian hushed him.

Soon they saw a tall figure squeezing himself through the opening. He held a torch, but the beam did not fall on the two boys.

The man stooped as he walked further into the cave.

Without warning Sebastian dashed to the exit. The torch fell. The tall man heard the noise.

"Who's there?" the man growled as he turned.

Otieno stood stock still. He was numbed by shock. "How could his own brother abandon him to such a dangerous man?" he wondered.

In a flash Bad Bunde was at the cave's exit, but Sebastian was faster. He got out and ran frantically downhill. Disappointed, the tall man turned back to the cave. He had to move his booty. He was sure the boy would report him to the police.

"He is coming for me now," Otieno thought, his heart beating faster and faster as he heard Bunde's footsteps outside. If only the man had gone after Sebastian for a few more meters, it would have given him time to escape.

Suddenly Otieno had an idea. He scooped up two handfuls of sandy soil, then waited. The angry Bunde did not see him. Otieno threw the sand directly into his face, blinding him for a few moments. Startled, Bunde tried to get to his feet.

"Oh God, please help me!" Otieno mumbled a quick prayer.

The cave's roof was too low for a giant like Bunde. He banged his head on the rocky roof and slumped headlong onto the floor. Blood gushed from a deep cut on his head.

In a flash, Otieno grabbed the man's torch. He rushed for the pieces of rope which Sebastian had untied earlier. The man was still motionless. With skillful hands, Otieno tied the man's hands with a fisherman's knot, then stuffed his handkerchief into the criminal's mouth.

"I guess Mr. Sikauti has never used this knot to tie a man!" Otieno chuckled as he remembered his scoutmaster.

Otieno ran all the way to Ngomeni Police Post.

"Sir, I've found him!" he exclaimed. The duty officer looked at him with little interest.

"Who is *him*?" he rasped.

"The drugs... the drugs-man. Hurry, he may escape!"

This caught the officer's attention. Soon Otieno and a group of policemen were at the cave. They found Bunde attempting to escape, but he was only crawling because he had lost so much blood and was very weak.

"Thank God you came running. We might have missed him!" one of the policemen said to Otieno.

An hour later, Sebastian arrived home. He had walked slowly for fear of what his mother would ask him about Otieno. He was surprised to see a police Land Rover and a big crowd of people.

"That is Otieno's voice," he muttered to himself. "How did he get here?"

His mother saw him.

"Sebastian, Sebastian, your brother is home! Rush, he has a story to tell you."

With an embarrassed smile, Sebastian listened as his brother told him about his feat. The police promised to deliver the reward by the end of the week.

Otieno was very excited, but mainly he was thankful to God for teaching him to be brave. His brother could never call him a coward again.

Peter Njoroge Mwaura, a Kenyan, works with the Assemblies of God Literature Centre in Nairobi, where he prepares Sunday School materials for his church. He wrote this story in 1992 at a Writing for Children Workshop given by Phoebe Mugo at Daystar University College in Kenya.

Elaine's African Christmas

Mabel Segun

Mrs. Lolade Ajayi backed the maroon Volvo out of the garage and stopped beside the girls waiting in the driveway. One was her twelve-year-old daughter Omowunmi, who was usually called Wunmi. The other girl, Elaine, was the same age. They both had a slender build but Wunmi was slightly taller. Elaine was a blond with startling blue eyes while Wunmi was very dark with brown eyes. Wunmi's grandmother always called her *Adumaadan* because of the smoothness of her dark skin.

"Hop in, girls," Mrs. Ajayi said. "I want to get to the shops before they become too crowded."

"Yes, Mummy," said Wunmi.

"Yes, Auntie Lolade," said Elaine.

Wunmi had told Elaine that in Nigeria children called older persons "auntie" and "uncle" as a sign of respect.

Wunmi opened the back door and the two girls got in.

Mrs. Ajayi turned her head and jokingly said, "Now I've become your chauffeur."

Wunmi said, "Would you like Elaine to come to the front? I don't mind."

"That's not a bad idea," Mrs. Ajayi said. "This is Elaine's

first visit here to Nigeria and she can see better from the front seat."

As Mrs. Ajayi drove, she explained all the sights, often in a funny way. Elaine really liked Auntie Lolade, a slightly plump but very active woman just over forty. She had a lively voice. Elaine had not yet met Dr. Ajayi, who was attending a medical conference in Ilorin.

Elaine Brown had come from New Jersey to spend Christmas holidays with the Ajayi family. Many years ago, Mrs. Ajayi had stayed with the Browns in the United States while training as a children's book editor. A firm and lasting friendship had sprung up. Last year, Mrs. Ajayi and Wunmi had spent Thanksgiving with the Browns. Elaine and Wunmi became friends and so it was arranged that Elaine should visit the Ajayis this year.

Elaine had always enjoyed Christmas shopping, but found it even more interesting here, for they visited not only the department stores but also the local markets. Best of all was Eko Bridge, one of the three bridges that link Lagos Island with mainland Lagos. There, people took advantage of the stop-go, crawl-stop movement of cars and buses to sell their wares. Elaine had never seen anything like it. All sorts of articles were on sale, from wall clocks to kitchen utensils, from dishes to car parts, from children's clothes and books and toys to Christmas decorations.

Mrs. Ajayi shooed away a youth of about fifteen who was shoving an iron under her nose. "I never buy electrical goods on the bridge," she explained to Elaine. "How would I know they work?"

But she bought some baby toys from another vendor. "For my nieces and nephews," she told Elaine.

The department stores had all been decorated for Christmas. Mothers with young children were lining up to see Father Christmas. He wore a costume and his beard was made of cotton.

After they bought many things to eat and drink, two

shop assistants carried the crates and cartons to their Volvo in the car park.

Mrs. Ajayi then led the way through a maze of streets till she came to a cloth market where she bought beautiful tie-and-dye and batik dress materials. Then they went to the wholesale market where Mrs. Ajayi bought cartons of tinned milk, sugar, tinned tomatoes and sardines. She also bought half a bag of rice. Watching her bargain over each item, Elaine wondered who in the end was the winner and who was the loser. Mrs. Ajayi told her there was neither winner nor loser when both parties were used to the game.

By the time they had finished their shopping, the car was crammed full. Mrs. Ajayi drove back to the house. David the houseboy helped the girls unload the purchases.

Elaine was so tired both from the shopping and the excitement that she went to lie on her bed with a book. But soon the book fell from her hands. She was asleep. The sound of the bedroom door opening woke her up. Wunmi came in and said, "It's time for lunch." Elaine realized that she was very hungry.

They had rice and chicken stew for lunch. Elaine kept wondering when Mrs. Ajayi was going to buy the Christmas turkey. Or didn't Nigerians eat turkey at their Christmas dinner? She decided to ask Wunmi when they were back in their room.

"Sure," Wunmi replied. "We always have a turkey at Christmas. Daddy has booked one. He'll bring it with him from Ilorin. We'll eat goat meat too. It's very tasty. One of Daddy's friends from the north always sends him a ram at Christmas."

Elaine secretly wondered how the Ajayi family could eat a whole turkey and a whole goat at Christmas but said nothing.

Two days later Dr. Ajayi came back from Ilorin. He was a tall, quiet man who greeted Elaine warmly. He asked about her parents and whether she was enjoying her visit, then disappeared into his study.

Elaine was shocked when she saw the turkey he had brought. It was a live one! Elaine was fascinated by its antics as it strutted about in the backyard, fanning out its tail feathers with an explosive sound and making funny sounds in its throat. A thought occurred to her. Who was going to kill it? She was sure she could never watch it being killed. But she wouldn't mind eating it. She hoped Mrs. Ajayi could stuff turkey the way her mother did.

Wunmi saw Elaine watching the turkey. She seemed to guess her thoughts and said, "I bet you're thinking of turkey stuffing and cranberry sauce. I'd better warn you. There won't be any. Mummy's going to cook it the Nigerian way."

Elaine was disappointed. How would turkey taste without the stuffing? Another disturbing thought came to her mind. Maybe they wouldn't have a Christmas tree. All the trees she had seen in Lagos were tropical trees, nothing like a fir, or spruce or pine. She was beginning to think Christmas would be deadly dull.

The next day Biodun arrived. He was Wunmi's eighteen-year-old brother who was studying at the University of Ibadan. He was an athletic young man, tall like his father and lively like his mother.

"Hi, Elaine," he said when she was introduced. Then he turned to Wunmi. "So what are we doing this year?"

Seeing the puzzled look on Elaine's face, Wunmi explained. "On Christmas Day there is a combined adult and Sunday School service in our church, with special presentations. Last year Biodun wrote a nativity play. It was all in mime and nobody had to learn a single line!"

Biodun said, "I've thought of something different for this year."

"What is it?" Elaine and Wunmi asked together.

"A Yoruba carol. It's very simple but delightful, because you accompany the singing with three instruments—a gong, a drum and the *sekere* rattle. I'll sing it."

Agogo ma nro o
Ilu ma ndun o
Sekere so wowo
Chorus:
Ojo ayo leyi ma je fun wa
Keresimesi odun de,
Odun Oluwa
Keresimesi odun de.

"You see, as you mention each instrument, you play it, and when you get to the chorus, you combine the three instruments."

Elaine had listened with rapt attention. "It sounds lovely, but what do the words mean?" she asked.

Biodun translated: "Bells are ringing, drums are rolling, gourds are rattling." And the chorus is:

This is a day of joy for us
Festive Christmas is here,
The Festival of our Lord
Joyful Christmas is here.

"So 'Keresimesi' is 'Christmas?' It's more musical than our word."

"Now which instrument would you like to play?" Biodun asked.

"I think I'll shake the rattle," Wunmi said.

"That leaves me with the talking drum. I knew it would happen that way," said Biodun.

"I bet you'll love showing off with the talking drum."

Elaine asked, "Do I have to sing too?"

"Of course," Biodun said.

Elaine looked dismayed. "Suppose I forget the words? I'm not sure I can sing in Yoruba."

"Nonsense, sure you can," said Biodun. "You only have to put your mind to it."

"Tell you what, Biodun," Wunmi put in. "Why don't you put the whole song on tape? Elaine can then play it over and over and learn her part."

"That's a wonderful idea, Wunmi," said Elaine, and she began to look enthusiastic.

"We'll have rehearsal from time to time," Biodun said.

"Yes, Mr. Choirmaster," Wunmi said.

Elaine woke up one morning to bleating sounds she could not at first identify. She looked out of the bedroom window and saw a large ram with curved horns tethered to one of the posts carrying the clothesline. It must have been brought last night after she and Wunmi went to bed.

The following morning, Dr. Ajayi hired a pickup truck and went with Biodun to fetch the Christmas tree. It was really a casuarina tree he had ordered from Agege Gardens eight months before. Elaine was delighted when she saw it. It was not the kind she was used to, but it had the right shape of a Christmas tree. Wunmi too was happy. "It's taller than last year's so we can hang more ornaments. There was plenty of rain this year."

"And now there's no rain at all, only *harmattan* haze and dust," Elaine said. She had discovered that Nigeria had only two seasons: rainy and dry. During the dry season, the cold, dry wind blew fine greyish dust from the Sahara Desert and one had to dust the furniture twice a day.

On the morning of Christmas Eve, Mrs. Ajayi and the two girls went over to the church, which was really the Assembly Hall of the University of Lagos Teaching Hospital.

"I thought you'd like to see the decorating of the hall, Elaine," Mrs. Ajayi said. Just then, they heard a crunching sound on the gravel. A big truck came to a stop beside the building. Two men leaped down and started unloading palm branches, laying them all over the ground. When the truck was empty, they bent down and began to braid each palm branch, tying up the ends with one of the ribs. They then carried the braided branches to the many doors of the hall, making arches over each one.

"It's a special art," Mrs. Ajayi said. "The 'braids' must

not be too tight or you can't push the flower stalks in. And they mustn't be loose or the flowers will fall out."

Elaine tried to visualize what Mrs. Ajayi was talking about but couldn't.

When they got back home, the ram had been killed, skinned and cut in pieces. Elaine thought, "That's why Auntie Lolade took us to the church, so I wouldn't see the ram being killed." Wunmi told her some men usually were hired to do the job. Dr. Ajayi supervised their work.

Some female relatives were washing the meat, while others were cutting up onions, tomatoes and peppers. Huge iron pots stood on stone tripods with firewood underneath. The fires were still smoking because they had just been lit.

The women worked all day and half the night, chatting away. Their children ran about and sometimes they had to rescue the toddlers when they went near the fire.

In the evening the girls decorated the Christmas tree which had been placed in an iron bucket half filled with water. The tree was wedged with large stones and the whole bucket covered with gift wrap. Dr. Ajayi had fixed the twinkly lights while they were at the church. Elaine and Wunmi arranged shimmering garlands around the tree, then tied small bells and balls to the branches with black thread. Finally, they hung "icicles" on the branches. The tree looked wonderful when the lights were switched on.

"Auntie Lolade, Auntie Lolade," Elaine called. "Come and look at the tree, it's beautiful!"

Mrs. Ajayi popped her head through the kitchen door, her hands wet from seasoning the turkey which had been killed by David. "You've done a wonderful job, girls," she said and went back to the kitchen. She finished the seasoning and put the turkey in the refrigerator.

Dr. Ajayi put on some Christmas records and the family sat in the sitting/dining room singing along with the record. From time to time Mrs. Ajayi went out to see what the women were doing. The whole area was full of Christmas sounds: fireworks, drumming and singing. Twice some neighborhood children came up to the house led by a small masquerade. They made music by beating empty food tins with sticks. Dr. Ajayi gave each group some money and each time the group chanted, "God bless this house and all that live in it. Thank you, sir."

When all the cooking had been done except for the rice and the turkey, the women packed everything into the kitchen, then went and slept in the boys' quarters. But by then Elaine and Wunmi were asleep.

Elaine woke up late because she was so tired from the previous night. As she entered the sitting/dining room to look again at the Christmas tree, Mrs. Ajayi came in from outside and announced brightly, "We've put in the flowers." Elaine wondered if she ever got tired.

After breakfast, Elaine got yet another surprise. On her neatly made-up bed was a pale blue batik outfit with a pattern that matched her eyes. A similar outfit was on Wunmi's bed, but it was a pastel green. Wunmi came in. She said, "Here, sisters wear identical clothes when they go out to festivals. But since you westerners don't like doing that, Mum thought she should use the same material, have it sewn the same style but have different colors."

"It's so pretty!" Elaine said, and went to hug Wunmi. "Auntie Lolade is super." She paused, then added, "But when were they sewn?"

"You remember that day we went shopping? You were so tired you went off to sleep. So Mum and I rushed off to the dressmaker. Since we're both the same size, she only had to take my measurements."

"I love your Mum, Wunmi. I must thank her right now."

They had breakfast, dressed quickly and went to church in two cars—Dr. Ajayi's Mercedes Benz, and Mrs. Ajayi's Volvo—so their clothes would not get crushed.

Elaine gasped when she saw the hall. The flowers stuck out cheerfully from the green palm weave: so many different kinds of flowers, every color of the rainbow!

The Ajayis went to their places and the combined service began. Just before the sermon the Sunday School children sang some choruses, then it was time for the Ajayi children to sing their Yoruba carol. Elaine's heart beat wildly as their names were announced. Wunmi seemed to sense her nervousness and placed her hand over Elaine's.

When they got up to stand in front of the congregation, some young children called out "oyinbo girl" on seeing a white girl among the trio. But everything went well, and as they sang the chorus with the three instruments combined, the congregation swayed to the rhythm of the music and clapped their hands.

When they finished and started going back to their seats, a round of applause followed them. The whole scene reminded Elaine of the psalm: "Let us make a joyful noise to the Lord." Elaine made a vow: She must teach this lovely carol to the young people in her church in New Jersey.

The service ended at noon and the Ajayis hurried home. Mrs. Ajayi had to supervise the giving of food to neighbors, relatives and friends. Elaine and Wunmi acted as couriers and were given some money for their trouble. The Ajayis also received dishes of food. The girls and Biodun were kept busy turning out food into their own dishes, washing and returning the dishes in which food had been brought.

Christmas dinner was a real treat. Elaine wondered why she thought the only way to cook turkey was by stuffing it. The meat had been stewed until it became juicy, then fried in hot groundnut oil until it became brown. The spices tasted wonderful and made Elaine's mouth water. The jolof rice was rich in ingredients and had an inviting pink-red look. There was also a bean paste mixed with groundnut oil, peppers, onions, tomatoes, ground crayfish, and bits of fresh shrimp and liver. By the time Mrs. Ajayi brought out the Christmas cake she had baked two weeks before, everybody was full and pleaded that it be kept until later.

People came to visit the Ajayis and they visited in return. In this way, Elaine was able to meet members of the Ajayis' extended family. When they got to Wunmi's grandmother's place, Elaine carefully did as Wunmi did, kneeling to greet the old woman. Wunmi's grandmother recited the granddaughter's praise poem of her pet name *Agbeke*. There and then she renamed Elaine *Tokunbo* (she who comes from overseas), and invented a praise poem for the name.

What beautiful memories Elaine would carry back to her country of her first African Christmas!

Mabel Segun of Lagos wrote this story especially for Friendship Press. President of the Children's Literature Association of Nigeria and director of the Children's Literature Documentation and Research Centre, she is internationally known as a children's writer, editor and teacher.

Glossary

Afrikaans	official South African language developed from 17th century Dutch colonists
batik	method of hand-printing fabrics, by coating with wax the parts not to be dyed
booby trap	bomb or land mine, buried but with a small triggering device above ground
booked	British term meaning reserved in advance
compound	group of buildings, often surrounded by a wall or fence
debe	large tin used as a measure, like a bushel
groundnuts	peanuts; staple crop in many parts of Africa
houseboy	British colonial term for servant, still in use today; house servants and gardeners sleep in a separate building on the compound known as **boys' quarters.**
harmattan	dust-laden wind on Atlantic coast of Africa in certain seasons
jolof	relating to the Wolof people and language of West Africa
juju	harmful magic or witchcraft, primarily in West Africa
jute	plant fiber used in making burlap sacks and twine
kente	special cloth, primarily in Ghana, woven in geometric patterns of red, green, gold, and black
kitenge	brightly colored rectangle of cloth, illustrated with African art, used for a dress or skirt (plural, **vitenge**)
lorry	British term for open truck
maize	corn; a staple crop, whose kernels are ground into meal or flour
mealie-cobs	corn cobs
millet	staple crop; a grass whose seeds are ground into flour
porridge	soft or soupy cereal made by boiling maize meal in water
sekere	rattle made from dried gourd with beads tied around it
shamba	small plot of land for cultivation
sisal	strong white fiber used for cords and twine
spirits	British term for turpentine
standard	British term for grade in school
torch	British term for flashlight
township	segregated community "reserved" for black South Africans
tie-and-dye	hand method of producing fabric designs by tying the portion not to be dyed
ugali	staple food made from maize flour; a stiff porridge
veld	grassland, with scattered shrubs or trees

A note on pronunciation: The unfamiliarity of African names may appear to make pronunciation difficult, but they almost always are pronounced the way they are spelled. Use the phonetic method, remember that the vowels **a, e, i, o,** and **u** are generally pronounced *ah, eh, ee, oh* and *oo*, and you'll be okay!